D1011120

Sweeney, Jacqueline.
Hester /
1999.
33305014628634
MI   09/13/00

WE CAN READ!™

HESTER

by Jacqueline Sweeney

photography by G. K. & Vikki Hart
photo illustration by Blind Mice Studio

BENCHMARK BOOKS

MARSHALL CAVENDISH
NEW YORK

SANTA CLARA COUNTY LIBRARY

3 3305 01462 8634

For all my Hesters —
Marian, Anandi, Joanne, Sadie, Nadine

With thanks to Daria Murphy, Reading Specialist,
K-8 English Language Arts Coordinator,
for reading this manuscript with care and for writing
the "We Can Read and Learn" activity guide.

Benchmark Books
Marshall Cavendish Corporation
99 White Plains Road
Tarrytown, New York 10591

Text copyright © 2000 by Jacqueline Sweeney
Photo illustrations copyright © 2000 by G. K. & Vikki Hart
and Mark & Kendra Empey

All rights reserved. No part of this book may be reproduced in any form
without written permission from the publisher.

Library of Congress Cataloging-in-Publication Data
Sweeney, Jacqueline.
Hester / Jacqueline Sweeney.
p.   cm. — (We can read!)
Summary: Hester the snake explains to her new animal friends how she sheds her
skin four times a year in order to grow.
ISBN 0-7614-0923-8 (lib. bdg.)
[1. Snakes—Fiction. 2. Animals—Fiction.]   I. Title.
II. Series: We can read! (Benchmark Books/Marshall Cavendish)
PZ7.S974255He   1999   [E]—dc21   98-43343 CIP   AC

Printed in Italy

1 3 5 6 4 2

Characters

Molly

 Gus

Tim

 Jim

Ron

 Ladybug

Hildy

 Eddie

Hester

"Look!" squeaked Molly.

"Over there — on Pond Rock!"

"I see it!" yelled Tim.

"It's white," grunted Gus.

"It's flapping," croaked Ron.

"Let's get closer," said Ladybug.

"I'll race you!" quacked Hildy.

Everyone started to run.

"It's huge!" cried Ladybug.

"It's small," said Hildy.

"It's smooth," said Molly, "and soft."

"Feels like paper," said Ron.

"Like plastic," said Tim.

Jim squinted. "Is it a cloud?"

"I see tiny stars!" said Gus.

"Diamonds," said Ladybug.

Hildy sang:

> Paper and plastic
>
> all in one.
>
> Shines like diamonds
>
> in the Sun.

No one heard
the snake's slow slide.
But *everyone* heard
HISS-*S*-*S*-S

"Eek!" shrieked Molly.
"Help!" squealed Tim.

"S-s-s-s-stop!" hissed Hester.

"Run!" cried Jim.

He ran right into her!

Molly fainted.

Gus hid in his shell.

"Don't be scared," said the snake.
"I'm Grandma Hester."
Her tongue flicked.

"And that's my skin."

"*Come back!*"

Slowly they moved closer.
"I shed my skin
FOUR times a year," said Hester.

"Why?" asked Ladybug.

Hester smiled.

"So I can grow," she said.

"Like when I lose my feathers?"
asked Hildy.

"When polliwogs lose their tails?"
asked Ron.

"Yes," said Hester.

"Aren't you too old to grow?"
asked Tim.

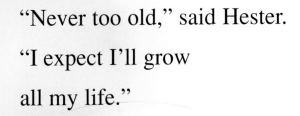

"Never too old," said Hester.
"I expect I'll grow
all my life."

The sun was low.

"Time to go," said Hester.

PLIP!

She slipped into the pond.

"Will you be *our* Grandma?" called Gus.

"Oh yes-s-s-s," said Hester.

"Will you visit me again?"

"Oh yes,"
said the friends.
"Yes-s-s-s!"

WE CAN READ AND LEARN

The following activities are designed to enhance literacy development. *Hester* can help children to build skills in vocabulary, phonics, and creative writing; to explore self-awareness; and to make connections between literature and other subject areas such as science and math.

HESTER'S CHALLENGE WORDS

Discuss the meanings of these words and use them to help children write a poem or to tell their own stories about Hester and her new friends.

croak	faint	flap	flick
grunt	polliwog	shed	shriek
smooth	soft	squeak	squeal
squint	startle	tiny	

FUN WITH PHONICS

Hester's Domino Game. Help children strengthen phonics skills by playing dominoes. You will need 3 X 5 index cards, a ruler, and a pencil or marker to make the dominoes. Divide the index cards in half by drawing a line down the middle of each card. On each side write either a short e word or a blend word. Have the children match a short e word or a blend word on their own card with a card that has been played. Create a domino snake! The first player to use all their dominoes wins.

Short e words:

Hester	never
expect	let's
get	everyone
feathers	help
shed	when
friends	yelled
yes	shell

Blend words:

grunted	grandma	grow
flapping	flicked	closer
cloud	started	stars
stop	small	smooth
smiled	plastic	plip
slow	slide	slowly
slipped	squinted	squeaked

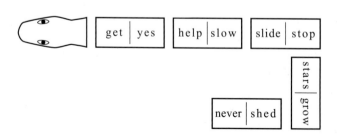

Slithery Snake Sentences. This story is filled with beautiful language and alliteration. Children can listen to an adult read the story and identify words that begin with the same sound, such as "grunted Gus" and "snakes slow slide." These phrases can be used as starting points to create alliterative sentences. Collect as many as possible and staple them together for a book of "slithery snake sentences." Be sure to have children illustrate each sentence.

CREATIVE WRITING

Hester Has Texture. Hester's skin is smooth like paper or plastic. It feels soft too. Describe how everyday objects with various textures feel. Find things that are as smooth as plastic, as soft as feathers, or as rough as sandpaper. Ask children to describe and compare objects in school or at home. They can put objects in a box or a bag and describe their textures using only their sense of touch. Children can use these experiences to write "texture poems." Have them write about objects, places, or people, describing them as Hester's friends described her skin in this story.

Snake Puppets. Using tube socks, create snake puppets that resemble Grandma Hester. Markings can be made with paint or colored tape strips. Glue on button eyes and a felt or fabric tongue. Children can use Grandma Hester to retell the story in their own words, remembering to sequence the events as they occurred.

SNAKE STUDIES

Help children to learn about snakes. Books from the library can be a source of information about how and why snakes like Hester shed their skin. Research various types of snakes. What kind of snake is Hester? Which snakes are poisonous? Which snakes live in your region? Young researchers can also be encouraged to explore other animal changes. Why do ducks lose their feathers? What happens to polliwogs? Each fact can be written on a narrow strip of paper and glued or taped together to create a super snake.

DIAMONDS IN THE SUN

Cut pieces of construction paper into a variety of shapes for children. Diamonds, stars, circles, squares, rectangles, triangles, ovals. . . . Each child can create a patterned snake using several geometric shapes. Children glue shapes down in a pattern on a large sheet of paper, creating their own unique patterns, such as triangle, diamond, triangle, diamond.

If you cut these same shapes into halves or quarters, you can introduce children to the concept of fractions. Fractions, or sections, can be put back together to create new shapes and snakes.

About the author

Jacqueline Sweeney has published children's poems and stories in many anthologies and magazines. An author for Writers in the Schools and for Alternative Literary Programs in Schools, she has written numerous professional books on creative methods for teaching writing. She lives in Stone Ridge, New York.

About the photo illustrations

The photo illustrations are the collaborative effort of photographers G. K. and Vikki Hart and Blind Mice Studio. Following Mark Empey's sketched story board, G. K. and Vikki Hart photograph each animal and element individually. The images are then scanned and manipulated, pixel by pixel, by Mark and Kendra Empey at Blind Mice Studio.

Each charming illustration may contain from 15 to 30 individual photographs.

All the animals that appear in this book were handled with love. The ladybugs and butterflies were set free in the garden, while the others have been returned to or adopted by loving homes.